A CHILD'S TREASURY
OF
ANIMAL
VERSE

A CHILD'S TREASURY
OF
ANIMAL
VERSE

COMPILED BY MARK DANIEL

Dial Books for Young Readers
New York

For Ann

Published by Dial Books for Young Readers
A Division of Penguin Books USA Inc.
375 Hudson Street
New York, New York 10014
Conceived and produced by Breslich & Foss, London
Copyright © 1989 by Breslich & Foss
All rights reserved
Printed and bound in China
Designed by Roger Daniels
D
3 5 7 9 10 8 6 4 2

Library of Congress Cataloging in Publication Data
A child's treasury of animal verse
compiled by Mark Daniel.
p.   cm.
Includes index.
Summary: An illustrated collection of rhymes, songs,
and poems about animals from Belloc, Rossetti, Wordsworth,
and other British and American writers of the nineteenth
and early twentieth century.
ISBN 0-8037-0606-5
1. Animals — Juvenile poetry. 2. Children's poetry, English.
3. Children's poetry, American. 1. Animals — Poetry. 2. English
poetry — Collections. 3. American poetry — Collections.
1. Daniel, Mark.
PR1195.A64C48 1989   821'.008'036—dc19   88-38276CIP   AC

The art for this book consists of full-color reproductions
of oil paintings from the Edwardian and Victorian eras, as well as
prints of black-and-white engravings from the same periods.
All color pictures are courtesy of
Fine Art Photographic Library, London,
except page 99 (Bridgeman Art Library).

Poems by Hilaire Belloc which appear in this
anthology are reprinted by kind permission of
Peters, Fraser & Dunlop Group Ltd.

CONTENTS

MAN'S
BEST
FRIENDS

Pussy can sit by the fire and sing,
Pussy can climb a tree,
Or play with a silly old cork and string
To 'muse herself, not me.
But I like Binkie my dog, because
He knows how to behave;
So, Binkie's the same as the first Friend was,
And I am the Man in the Cave.

Pussy will play Man-Friday till
It's time to wet her paw
And make her walk on the window-sill
(For the footprint Crusoe saw);
Then she fluffles her tail and mews,
And scratches and won't attend.
But Binkie will play whenever I choose,
And he is my true first friend.

Pussy will rub my knees with her head
Pretending she loves me hard;
But the very minute I go to bed
Pussy runs out in the yard,
And there she stays till the morning-light;
So I know it is only pretend;
But Binkie, he snores at my feet all night,
And he is my Firstest Friend!

RUDYARD KIPLING
Just So Stories, 1902

My dog's so furry I've not seen
His face for years and years:
His eyes are buried out of sight,
I only guess his ears.

When people ask me for his breed,
I do not know or care:
He has the beauty of them all
Hidden beneath his hair.

HERBERT ASQUITH

HURT NO LIVING THING

Hurt no living thing,
Ladybird nor butterfly,
Nor moth with dusty wing,
Nor cricket chirping cheerily,
Nor grasshopper, so light of leap,
Nor dancing gnat,
Nor beetle fat,
Nor harmless worms that creep.

CHRISTINA ROSSETTI
Sing-Song, 1872

THE CAT AND THE MOON

The cat went here and there
And the moon spun round like a top,
And the nearest kin of the moon,
The creeping cat, looked up.
Black Minnaloushe stared at the moon,
For, wander and wail as he would,
The pure cold light in the sky
Troubled his animal blood.
Minnaloushe runs in the grass
Lifting his delicate feet.
Do you dance, Minnaloushe, do you dance?
When two close kindred meet,
What better than call a dance?
Maybe the moon may learn,
Tired of that courtly fashion,
A new dance turn.
Minnaloushe creeps through the grass
From moonlit place to place,
The sacred moon overhead
Has taken a new phase.
Does Minnaloushe know that his pupils
Will pass from change to change,
And that from round to crescent,
From crescent to round they range?
Minnaloushe creeps through the grass
Alone, important and wise,
And lifts to the changing moon
His changing eyes.

W. B. YEATS
The Wild Swans at Coole, 1919

OLD MOTHER HUBBARD

Old Mother Hubbard
Went to the cupboard
To get her poor dog a bone,
But when she got there
The cupboard was bare
And so the poor dog had none.

She went to the baker's
To buy him some bread,
But when she came back
The poor dog was dead.

She went to the joiner's
To buy him a coffin,
But when she came back
The poor dog was laughing.

She took a clean dish
To get him some tripe,
But when she came back
He was smoking his pipe.

She went to the fish-man's
To buy him some fish,
And when she came back
He was licking the dish.

She went to the ale-house
To get him some beer,
But when she came back
The dog sat in a chair.

She went to the tavern
For white wine and red,
But when she came back
The dog stood on his head.

She went to the hatter's
To buy him a hat,
But when she came back
He was feeding the cat.

She went to the barber's
To buy him a wig,
But when she came back
He was dancing a jig.

She went to the tailor's
To buy him a coat,
But when she came back
He was riding a goat.

She went to the cobbler's
To buy him some shoes,
But when she came back
He was reading the news.

She went to the seamstress
To buy him some linen,
But when she came back
The dog was spinning.

She went to the hosier's
To buy him some hose,
But when she came back
He was dressed in his clothes.

The dame made a curtsy,
The dog made a bow;
The dame said, "Your servant,"
The dog said, "Bow wow."

ANON

THE KITTEN PLAYING WITH THE FALLING LEAVES

See the kitten on the wall
Sporting with the leaves that fall!
Withered leaves, one, two, and three,
From the lofty elder-tree.
Through the calm and frosty air
Of this morning bright and fair
Eddying round and round they sink
Softly, slowly. — One might think,
From the motions that are made,
Every little leaf conveyed
Some small fairy, hither tending,
To this lower world descending.
— But the kitten how she starts!
Crouches, stretches, paws, and darts:
First at one, and then its fellow,
Just as light, and just as yellow:
There are many now — now one —
Now they stop and there are none.
What intentness of desire
In her up-turned eye of fire!
With a tiger-leap half way,
Now she meets the coming prey.
Lets it go at last, and then
Has it in her power again.

WILLIAM WORDSWORTH

Who's that ringing at the front door bell?"
Miau! Miau! Miau!
"I'm a little Pussy Cat and I'm not very well!"
Miau! Miau! Miau!
"Then rub your nose in a bit of mutton fat."
Miau! Miau! Miau!
"For that's the way to cure a little Pussy Cat."
Miau! Miau! Miau!

D'ARCY WENTWORTH THOMPSON
Nursery Nonsense, 1864

THE PEKINESE

The Pekinese
  Adore their ease
And slumber like the dead;
In comfort curled
They view the world
As one unending bed.

E. V. LUCAS

There was a little dog, and he had a little tail,
  And he used to wag, wag, wag it.
But whenever he was sad because he had been bad,
On the ground he would drag, drag, drag it.

He had a little nose, as of course you would suppose,
And on it was a muz-muz-muzzle,
And to get it off he'd try till a tear stood in his eye,
But he found it a puz-puz-puzzle.

ANON

There was a man, and his name was Dob,
  And he had a wife, and her name was Mob,
And he had a dog, and he called it Cob,
And she had a cat called Chitterabob.

"Cob!," calls Dob.
"Chitterabob!," calls Mob.
Cob was Dob's dog.
Chitterabob Mob's cat.

ANON

HIS APOLOGIES

Master, this is Thy Servant. He is rising eight
weeks old.
He is mainly Head and Tummy. His legs are
uncontrolled.
But Thou hast forgiven his ugliness, and settled him
on thy knee...
Art Thou content with Thy Servant? He is *very*
comfy with Thee.

Master, behold a Sinner? He hath done grievous
wrong.
He hath defiled Thy Premises through being kept in
too long.
Wherefore his nose has been rubbed in the dirt, and
his self-respect has been bruised.
Master, pardon Thy Sinner, and see he is properly
loosed.

Master — again Thy Sinner! This that was once Thy
Shoe,
He hath found and taken and carried aside, as fitting
matter to chew.
Now there is neither blacking nor tongue, and the
Housemaid has us in toe.
Master, remember Thy Servant is young,
and tell her to let him go!

Master, behold Thy Servant! Strange children came
    to play
And because they fought to caress him, Thy Servant
    wentedst away.
But now that the Little Beasts have gone, he has
    returned to see
(Brushed — with his Sunday collar on —) what they
    left over from tea.

Master, pity Thy Servant! He is deaf and three parts
    blind,
He cannot catch Thy Commandments. He cannot
    read Thy Mind.
Oh, leave him not in his loneliness; nor make him
    that kitten's scorn.
He has had none other God than Thee since the year
    that he was born!

Lord, look down on Thy Servant! Bad things have
    come to pass,
There is no heat in the midday sun nor health in the
    wayside grass.
His bones are full of an old disease — his torments
    run and increase.
Lord, make haste with Thy Lightnings, and grant
    him a quick release!

               RUDYARD KIPLING
            Thy Servant A Dog, 1930.

Pussy cat sits by the fire;
    How did she come there?
In walks the little dog,
Says, "Pussy! Are you there?"

"How do you do, Mistress Pussy?
Mistress Pussy, how d'ye do?"
"I thank you kindly, little dog,
I fare as well as you!"

ANON

CATS OF KILKENNY

There once were two cats of Kilkenny;
 Each thought there was one cat too many;
So they fought and they fit,
And they scratched and they bit,
Till, excepting their nails
And the tips of their tails,
Instead of two cats, there weren't any.

ANON

THE CAT OF CATS

I am the cat of cats. I am
 The everlasting cat!
Cunning, and old, and sleek as jam,
The everlasting cat!
I hunt the vermin in the night —
The everlasting cat!
For I see best without the light —
The everlasting cat!

WILLIAM BRIGHTY RANDS
Good Words for the Young, 1868

Dame Trot and her cat
Sat down for to chat;
The Dame sat on this side,
And Puss sat on that.

"Puss," says the Dame,
"Can you catch a rat,
Or a mouse in the dark?"
"Purr," says the cat.

ANON

THE DINERS
IN THE KITCHEN

Our dog Fred
Et the bread

Our dog Dash
Et the hash

Our dog Pete
Et the meat

Our dog Davy
Et the gravy

Our dog Toffy
Et the coffee

Our dog Jake
Et the cake

Our dog Trip
Et the dip

And — the worst,
From the first —

Our dog Fido
Et the pie-dough

JAMES WHITCOMB RILEY
Rhymes of Childhood, 1891

IN
THE
FARMYARD

POTATO PEEL

Dearly loved children
Is it not a sin
When you peel potatoes,
To throw away the skin?
For the skin feeds pigs
And pigs feed you.
Dearly loved children,
Is this not true?

ANON

THE SHEEP

Lazy sheep, pray tell me why
In the grassy fields you lie,
Eating grass and daisies white,
From the morning till the night?
Everything can something do,
But what kind of use are you?

Nay, my little master, nay,
Do not serve me so, I pray;
Don't you see the wool that grows
On my back to make you clothes?
Cold, and very cold you'd get,
If I did not give you it.

Sure it seems a pleasant thing
To nip the daisies in the spring,
But many chilly nights I pass
On the cold and dewy grass,
Or pick a scanty dinner where
All the common's brown and bare.

Then the farmer comes at last,
When the merry spring is past,
And cuts my woolly coat away
To warm you in the winter's day;
Little master, this is why
In the grassy fields I lie.

ANN TAYLOR

Goosey, goosey, gander
Where shall I wander?
Upstairs, downstairs,
And in my lady's chamber.
There I met an old man
Who would not say his prayers;
I took him by the left leg
And threw him down the stairs.

ANON

Before the barn door crowing
The cock by hens attended,
His eyes around him throwing,
Stands for a while suspended;
Then one he singles from the crew,
And cheers the happy hen,
With how do you do, and how do you do,
And how do you do again.

JOHN GAY
Fables, 1738

Higgledy, piggledy, my black hen
She lays eggs for gentlemen;
Gentlemen come every day
To see what my black hen doth lay.

ANON

WHAT THE FARMYARD FOWL ARE SAYING

COCK: Lock the dairy door,
Lock the dairy door!

HEN: Chickle, chackle, chee,
I haven't got the key!

ANON

THE GOAT

There was a man, now please take note,
There was a man, who had a goat.
He lov'd that goat, indeed he did,
He lov'd that goat, just like a kid.

One day that goat felt frisk and fine,
Ate three red shirts from off the line.
The man he grabbed him by the back,
And tied him to a railroad track.

But when the train hove into sight,
The goat grew pale and green with fright.
He heaved a sigh, as if in pain,
Coughed up those shirts and flagged the train

ANON

THE COW

The friendly cow, all red and white,
I love with all my heart:
She gives me cream with all her might,
To eat with apple tart.

She wanders lowing here and there,
And yet she cannot stray,
All in the pleasant open air,
The pleasant light of day.

And blown by all the winds that pass
And wet with all the showers,
She walks among the meadow grass
And eats the meadow flowers.

ROBERT LOUIS STEVENSON
A Child's Garden of Verses, 1885

THE LAMB

Little lamb, who made thee?
Dost thou know who made thee,
Gave thee life, and bade thee feed
By the stream and o'er the mead.
Gave thee clothing of delight,
Softest clothing, woolly, bright;
Gave thee such a tender voice,
Making all the vales rejoice?
Little lamb, who made thee?
Dost thou know who made thee?

Little lamb, I'll tell thee;
Little lamb, I'll tell thee:
He is called by thy name,
For He calls Himself a Lamb;
He is meek, and He is mild,
He became a little child.
I a child, and thou a lamb,
We are called by His name.
Little lamb, God bless thee!
Little lamb, God bless thee!

WILLIAM BLAKE
Songs of Innocence, 1789

LAMBS AT PLAY

On the grassy banks
Lambkins at their pranks;
Woolly sisters, woolly brothers,
Jumping off their feet
While their woolly mothers
Watch by them and bleat.

CHRISTINA ROSSETTI
Sing-Song, 1872

A FRISKY LAMB

A frisky lamb
And a frisky child
Playing their pranks
In a cowslip meadow:
The sky all blue
And the air all mild
And the fields all sun
And the lanes half shadow.

CHRISTINA ROSSETTI
Sing-Song, 1872

A FARMER'S BOY

They strolled down the lane together,
The sky was studded with stars —
They reached the gate in silence
And he lifted down the bars —
She neither smiled nor thanked him
Because she knew not how;
For he was just a farmer's boy
And she was a jersey cow.

ANON

DUCKS' DITTY

All along the backwater,
Through the rushes tall,
Ducks are a-dabbling,
Up tails all!

Ducks' tails, drakes' tails,
Yellow feet a-quiver,
Yellow bills all out of sight
Busy in the river!

Slushy green undergrowth
Where the roach swim —
Here we keep our larder,
Cool and full and dim!

Every one for what he likes!
We like to be
Heads down, tails up,
Dabbling free!

High in the blue above
Swifts whirl and call —
We are down a-dabbling,
Up tails all!

KENNETH GRAHAME
The Wind In The Willows, 1908

THE ROBIN AND THE COWS

The robin sings in the elm;
   The cattle stand beneath,
Sedate and grave with great brown eyes,
And fragrant meadow-breath.

They listen to the flattered bird,
The wise-looking, stupid things!
And they never understand a word
Of all the robin sings.

WILLIAM DEAN HOWELLS

PIGS

Do look at those pigs as they lie in the straw,"
Said Dick to his father one day;
"They keep eating longer than I ever saw,
What nasty fat gluttons are they."

"I see they are feasting," his father reply'd,
"They eat a great deal, I allow;
But let us remember, before we deride,
'Tis the nature, my dear, of a sow.

"But when a great boy, such as you, my dear Dick,
Does nothing but eat all the day,
And keeps sucking good things till he makes himself
    sick,
What a glutton! indeed, we may say.

"When plumcake and sugar for ever he picks,
And sweetmeats, and comfits, and figs;
Pray let him get rid of his own nasty tricks,
And then he may laugh at the pigs."

JANE TAYLOR

BILLY GOAT

There was a young goat named Billy
Who was more than a little bit silly.
They sent him to school
But he just played the fool
And ate satchels and books willy-nilly.

ANON

Little Bo-peep has lost her sheep,
And can't tell where to find them;
Leave them alone, and they'll come home,
And bring their tails behind them.

Little Bo-peep fell fast asleep,
And dreamt she heard them bleating;
But when she awoke, she found it a joke,
For they were still a-fleeting.

Then up she took her little crook,
Determin'd for to find them;
She found them indeed, but it made her heart bleed,
For they'd left all their tails behind 'em.

ANON

Cushy cow bonny, let down thy milk,
And I will give thee a gown of silk;
A gown of silk and a silver tee,
If thou wilt let down thy milk to me.

ANON

THE COW

Thank you, pretty cow, that made
Pleasant milk, to soak my bread;
Every day, and every night,
Warm, and fresh, and sweet, and white.

Do not chew the hemlock rank,
Growing on the weedy bank;
But the yellow cowslips eat,
They will make it very sweet.

Where the purple violet grows,
Where the bubbling water flows,
Where the grass is fresh and fine,
Pretty cow, go there and dine.

ANN and JANE TAYLOR

FIVE LITTLE CHICKENS

Said the first little chicken,
With a queer little squirm,
"Oh, I wish I could find
A fat little worm!"

Said the next little chicken,
With an odd little shrug,
"Oh, I wish I could find
A fat little bug!"

Said the third little chicken,
With a sharp little squeal,
"Oh, I wish I could find
Some nice yellow meal!"

Said the fourth little chicken,
With a small sigh of grief,
"Oh, I wish I could find
A green little leaf!"

Said the fifth little chicken,
With a faint little moan,
"Oh, I wish I could find
A wee gravel stone!"

"Now, see here," said the mother,
From the green garden-patch,
"If you want any breakfast,
You must come here and scratch."

ANON

THE COW AND THE ASS

Beside a green meadow a stream used to flow,
So clear, you might see the white pebbles below;
To this cooling brook, the warm cattle would stray,
To stand in the shade on a hot summer's day.

A cow quite oppressed by the heat of the sun,
Came here to refresh as she often had done;
And, standing quite still, stooping over the stream
Was musing, perhaps — or perhaps she might
    dream.

But soon a brown ass of respectable look
Came trotting up also to taste of the brook,
And to nibble a few of the daisies and grass.
"How d'ye do?" said the cow. "How d'ye do?" said the
    ass.

"Take a seat!" said the cow, gently waving her hand.
"By no means, dear madam," said he, "while you
    stand!"
Then, stooping to drink, with a very low bow,
"Ma'am, your health!" said the ass.
"Thank you, sir," said the cow.

ANN and JANE TAYLOR

Cackle, cackle, Mother Goose,
Have you any feathers loose?
Truly have I, pretty fellow,
Half enough to fill a pillow.
Here are quills, take one or two,
And down to make a bed for you.

ANON

ALL
CREATURES
GREAT...

THE ELEPHANT

Here comes the elephant
Swaying along
With his cargo of children
All singing a song:
To the tinkle of laughter
He goes on his way,
And his cargo of children
Have crowned him with may.

His legs are in leather
And padded his toes;
He can root up an oak
With a whisk of his nose;
With a wave of his trunk
And a turn of his chin
He can pull down a house,
Or pick up a pin.
Beneath his grey forehead
A little eye peers;
Of what is he thinking
Between those wide ears?
What does he feel?

If he wished to tease,
He could twirl his keeper
Over the trees;
If he were not kind,
He could play cup and ball
With Robert and Helen,
And Uncle Paul;

But that grey forehead,
Those crinkled ears,
Have learned to be kind
In a hundred years:
And so with the children
He goes on his way
To the tinkle of laughter
And crowned with the may.

HERBERT ASQUITH

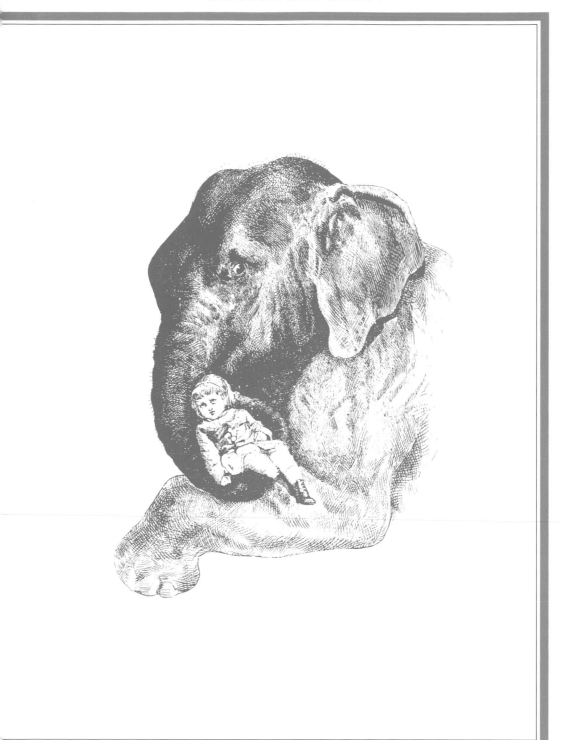

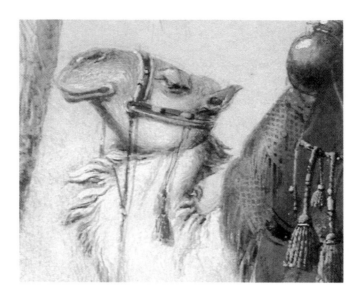

THE CAMEL'S LAMENT

Canary-birds feed on sugar and seed,
  Parrots have crackers to crunch;
And as for the poodles, they tell me the noodles
Have chickens and cream for their lunch.
But there's never a question
About MY digestion —
Anything does for me!

"Cats, you're aware, can repose in a chair,
Chickens can roost upon rails;
Puppies are able to sleep in a stable,
And oysters can slumber in pails.
But no one supposes
A poor Camel dozes —
Any place does for me!

"Lambs are enclosed where it's never exposed.
Coops are constructed for hens;
Kittens are treated to houses well heated,
And pigs are protected by pens.
But a Camel comes handy
Wherever it's sandy —
Anywhere does for me!

"People would laugh if you rode a giraffe,
Or mounted the back of an ox;
It's nobody's habit to ride on a rabbit,
Or try to bestraddle a fox.
But as for a Camel, he's
Ridden by families —
Any load does for me!

"A snake is as round as a hole in the ground,
And weasels are wavy and sleek;
And no alligator could ever be straighter
Than lizards that live in a creek.
But a Camel's all lumpy
And bumpy and humpy —
ANY shape does for me!"

CHARLES EDWARD CARRYL
The Admiral's Caravan, 1892

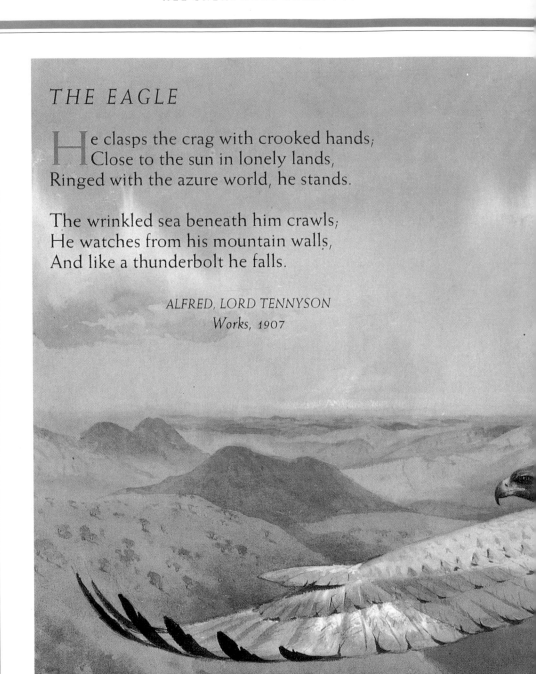

THE EAGLE

He clasps the crag with crooked hands;
Close to the sun in lonely lands,
Ringed with the azure world, he stands.

The wrinkled sea beneath him crawls;
He watches from his mountain walls,
And like a thunderbolt he falls.

ALFRED, LORD TENNYSON
Works, 1907

THE PELICAN CHORUS

King and Queen of the Pelicans we;
No other Birds so grand we see!
None but we have feet like fins!
With lovely leathery throats and chins!
    Ploffskin, Pluffskin, Pelican jee!
    We think no Birds so happy as we!
    Plumpskin, Ploshkin, Pelican jill!
    We think so then, and we thought so still!

We live on the Nile. The Nile we love.
By night we sleep on cliffs above;
By day we fish, and at eve we stand
On long bare islands of yellow sand.
And when the sun sinks slowly down
And the great rockwalls grow dark and brown
And the purple river rolls fast and dim,
And the ivory Ibis starlike skim,
Wing to wing we dance around –
Stamping our feet with a flumpy sound, –
Opening our mouths as Pelicans ought,
And this is the song we nightly snort;
    Ploffskin, Pluffskin, Pelican jee! —
    We think no Birds so happy as we!
    Plumpskin, Ploshkin, Pelican jill!
    We think so then, and we thought so still!

EDWARD LEAR
Laughable Lyrics, 1877

THE CROCODILE

How doth the little crocodile
Improve his shining tail
And pour the waters of the Nile
On every golden scale!

How cheerfully he seems to grin,
How neatly spreads his claws,
And welcomes little fishes in
With gently smiling jaws!

LEWIS CARROLL
Alice's Adventures in Wonderland, 1865

If you should meet a crocodile,
Don't take a stick and poke him;
Ignore the welcome of his smile,
Be careful not to stroke him.
For as he sleeps upon the Nile,
He thinner gets and thinner;
And where'er you meet a crocodile,
He's ready for his dinner.

ANON

THE LION

The Lion, the Lion, he dwells in the waste,
  He has a big head and a very small waist;
But his shoulders are stark, and his jaws they are
  grim,
And a good little child will not play with him.

HILAIRE BELLOC
The Bad Child's Book of Beasts, 1896

THE YAK

As a friend to the children, commend me the yak;
You will find it exactly the thing:
It will carry and fetch, you can ride on its back,
Or lead it about with a string.

The Tartar who dwells in the plains of Tibet
(A desolate region of snow),
Has for centuries made it a nursery pet,
And surely the Tartar should know!

Then tell your papa where the yak can be got,
And if he is awfully rich,
He will buy you the creature — or else he will not:
I cannot be positive which.

HILAIRE BELLOC
A Bad Child's Book of Beasts, 1896

I asked my mother for fifty cents
To see the elephant jump the fence.
He jumped so high he touched the sky
And never came back till the Fourth of July.

ANON

THE NYMPH AND HER FAWN

With sweetest milk and sugar first
I it at my own fingers nursed;
And as it grew, so every day
It wax'd more white and sweet than they —
It had so sweet a breath! and oft
I blush'd to see its foot more soft
And white — shall I say? — than my hand,
Nay, any lady's of the land!

It is a wondrous thing how fleet
'Twas on those little silver feet:
With what a pretty skipping grace
It oft would challenge me the race: —
And when't had left me far away
'Twould stay, and run again, and stay:
For it was nimbler much than hinds,
And trod as if on the four winds.

ANDREW MARVELL
Miscellaneous Poems, 1681

Hast thou given the horse strength? hast thou clothed his neck with thunder?

Canst thou make him afraid as a grasshopper? The glory of his nostrils *is* terrible.

He paweth in the valley, and rejoiceth in *his* strength: he goeth on to meet the armed men.

He mocketh at fear, and is not affrighted; neither turneth he back from the sword.

The quiver rattleth against him, the glittering spear and the shield.

He swalloweth the ground with fierceness and rage: neither believeth he that *it is* the sound of the trumpet.

He saith among the trumpets, Ha, ha; and he smelleth the battle afar off, the thunder of the captains, and the shouting.

JOB, CHAPTER 39, Verses 19-25

AT THE ZOO

First I saw the white bear, then I saw the black;
    Then I saw the camel with a hump upon his back;
Then I saw the grey wolf, with mutton in his maw;
Then I saw the wombat waddle in the straw;
Then I saw the elephant a-waving of his trunk;
Then I saw the monkeys — mercy, how unpleasantly
    they — smelt!

WILLIAM MAKEPEACE THACKERAY
Works, 1879

Fuzzy Wuzzy was a bear,
    A bear was Fuzzy Wuzzy.
When Fuzzy Wuzzy lost his hair
He wasn't fuzzy, was he?

ANON

SEAL LULLABY

Oh, hush thee, my baby, the night is behind us,
   And black are the waters that sparkled so green
The moon o'er the combers, looks downward to
   find us
At rest in the hollows that rustle between.
Where billow meets billow, there soft be thy pillow;
Ah, weary wee flipperling, curl at thy ease!
The storm shall not wake thee, nor sharks overtake
   thee,
Asleep in the arms of the slow-swinging sea.

RUDYARD KIPLING
The Jungle Books, 1914

THE TYGER

Tyger! Tyger! burning bright
In the forests of the night,
What immortal hand or eye
Could frame thy fearful symmetry?

In what distant deeps or skies
Burnt the fire of thine eyes?
On what wings dare he aspire?
What the hand dare seize the fire?

And what shoulder, and what art,
Could twist the sinews of thy heart?
And when thy heart began to beat,
What dread hand? and what dread feet?

What the hammer? what the chain?
In what furnace was thy brain?
What the anvil? what dread grasp
Dare its deadly terrors clasp?

When the stars threw down their spears,
And watered Heaven with their tears,
Did he smile his work to see?
Did He who made the Lamb make thee?

Tyger! Tyger! burning bright
In the forests of the night,
What immortal hand or eye,
Dare frame thy fearful symmetry?

WILLIAM BLAKE
Songs of Experience, 1794

THE FLY-AWAY HORSE

Oh, a wonderful horse is the Fly-Away Horse —
Perhaps you have seen him before;
Perhaps, while you slept, his shadow has swept
Through the moonlight that floats on the floor.
For it's only at night, when the stars twinkle bright,
That the Fly-Away Horse, with a neigh
And a pull at his rein and a toss of his mane,
Is up on his heels and away!
The Moon in the sky,
As he gallopeth by,
Cries: "Oh! what a marvellous sight!"
And the Stars in dismay
Hide their faces away
In the lap of old Grandmother Night.

Off! scamper to bed — you shall ride him to-night!
For, as soon as you've fallen asleep,
With a jubilant neigh he shall bear you away
Over forest and hillside and deep!
But tell us, my dear, all you see and you hear
In those beautiful lands over there,
Where the Fly-Away Horse wings his far-away
   course
With the wee one consigned to his care.
Then grandma will cry
In amazement: "Oh, my!"
And she'll think it could never be so.
And only we two
Shall know it is true —
You and I, little precious! shall know!

EUGENE FIELD
excerpt, Poems of Childhood, 1892

THE DONKEY

When fishes flew and forests walked
  And figs grew upon the thorn
Some moment when the moon was blood
Then surely I was born.

With monstrous head and sickening cry
And ears like errant wings,
The devil's walking parody
On all four-footed things.

The tattered outlaw of the earth,
Of ancient crooked will;
Starve, scourge, deride me; I am dumb,
I keep my secret still.

Fools! For I also had my hour;
One far fierce hour and sweet:
There was a shout about my ears,
And palms before my feet.

G. K. CHESTERTON
The Wild Knight, 1900

FALLOW DEER

One without looks in tonight
Through the curtain chink
From the sheet of glistening white;
One without looks in tonight
As we sit and think
By the fender-brink.

We do not discern those eyes
Watching in the snow;
Lit by lamps of rosy dyes
We do not discern those eyes
Wondering, aglow,
Fourfooted, tiptoe.

THOMAS HARDY
Late Lyrics, 1922

The lion and the unicorn
  Were fighting for the crown;
The lion beat the unicorn
All round the town.
Some gave them white bread,
And some gave them brown;
Some gave them plum cake,
And sent them out of town.

ANON

...AND
SMALL

A cat came fiddling out of a barn,
With a pair of bagpipes under her arm,
She could sing nothing but "Fiddle-de-de.
The mouse has married the bumblebee."
Pipe, cat — dance, mouse —
We'll have a wedding at our good house.

ANON

TO A SQUIRREL

Come play with me
Why should you run
Through the shaking tree
As though I'd a gun
To strike you dead?
When all I would do
Is to scratch your head
And let you go.

W. B. YEATS
The Wild Swans at Coole, 1919

THE FROG

Be kind and tender to the frog,
And do not call him names,
As "Slimy-Skin" or "Pollywog,"
Or likewise "Uncle James,"
Or "Gape-a-grin," or "Toad-gone-wrong,"
Or "Billy Bandy-Knees;"
The frog is justly sensitive
To epithets like these.

No animal will more repay
A treatment kind and fair,
At least, so lonely people say
Who keep a frog (and by the way,
They are extremely rare).

HILAIRE BELLOC
A Bad Child's Book of Beasts, 1896

THREE MICE

Three little mice walked into town,
  Their coats were grey, and their eyes were
brown.

Three little mice went down the street,
With woolwork slippers upon their feet.

Three little mice sat down to dine
On curranty bread and gooseberry wine.

Three little mice ate on and on,
Till every crumb of the bread was gone.

Three little mice, when the feast was done,
Crept home quietly one by one.

Three little mice went straight to bed,
And dreamt of crumbly, curranty bread.

CHARLOTTE DRUITT COLE

SNAKE

A narrow fellow in the grass
Occasionally rides;
You may have met him — did you not?
His notice sudden is.

The grass divides as with a comb,
A spotted shaft is seen,
And then it closes at your feet
And opens further on.

He likes a boggy acre,
A floor too cool for corn;
Yet when a child and barefoot,
I more than once at noon

Have passed, I thought, a whiplash
Upbraiding in the sun;
When, stooping to secure it,
It wrinkled and was gone.

Several of nature's people
I know, and they know me;
I feel for them a transport
Of cordiality

But never met this fellow,
Attended or alone,
Without a tighter breathing
And zero at the bone.

EMILY DICKINSON
Poems, 1890

THE SILENT SNAKE

The birds go fluttering in the air,
  The rabbits run and skip,
Brown squirrels race along the bough,
The May-flies rise and dip;
But, whilst these creatures play and leap,
The silent snake goes creepy-creep!

The birdies sing and whistle loud,
The busy insects hum,
The squirrels chat, the frogs say "croak!"
But the snake is always dumb.
With not a sound through grasses deep
The silent snake goes creepy-creep!

ANON

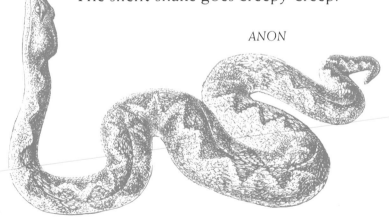

WE FISH

We fish, we fish, we merrily swim,
    We care not for friend nor for foe.
Our fins are stout,
Our tails are out,
As through the seas we go.

Fish, fish, we are fish with red gills;
Naught disturbs us, our blood is at zero:
We are buoyant because of our bags,
Being many, each fish is a hero.
We care not what is it, this life

That we follow, this phantom unknown;
To swim, it's exceedingly pleasant —
So swim away, making a foam.
This strange looking thing by our side,
Not for safety, around it we flee: —
Its shadow's so shady, that's all —
We only swim under its lee.
And as for the eels there above,
And as for the fowls of the air,
We care not for them nor their ways,
As we cheerily glide afar!

> HERMAN MELVILLE
> Mardi, 1849.

Little Tim Sprat
Had a pet rat,
In a tin cage with a wheel.
Said little Tim Sprat,
Each day to his rat:
"If hungry, my dear, you must squeal."

ANON

Croak!" said the Toad, "I'm hungry, I think;
Today I've had nothing to eat or to drink;
I'll crawl to a garden and jump through the pales,
And there I'll dine nicely on slugs and on snails."
"Ho, ho!" quoth the Frog, "is that what you mean?
Then I'll hop away to the next meadow stream;
There I will drink, and eat worms and slugs too,
And then I shall have a good dinner like you."

ANON

SIX LITTLE MICE

Six little mice sat down to spin;
Pussy passed by and she peeped in.
"What are you doing, my little men?"
"Weaving coats for gentlemen."
"Shall I come in and cut off your threads?"
"Oh, no, Mistress Pussy, you'd bite off our heads!"

ANON

THE MOUNTAIN AND THE SQUIRREL

The mountain and the squirrel
 Had a quarrel;
And the former called the latter "Little Prig."
Bun replied,
"You are doubtless very big;
But all sorts of things and weather
Must be taken in together,
To make up a year
And a sphere.
And I think it no disgrace
To occupy my place.
If I'm not so large as you,
You are not so small as I,
And not half so spry,
I'll not deny you make
A very pretty squirrel track;
Talents differ; all is well and wisely put;
If I cannot carry forests on my back,
Neither can you crack a nut."

RALPH WALDO EMERSON
Poems, 1914

FINGER PLAY

This little bunny said, "Let's play."
This little bunny said, "In the hay."
This one saw a man with a gun.
This one said, "This isn't fun."
This one said, "I'm off for a run."
Bang! went the gun,
They ran away
And didn't come back for a year and a day.

ANON

THE SQUIRREL

The squirrel, flippant, pert and full of play,
Drawn from his refuge in some lonely elm
That age or injury hath hollowed deep,
Where, on his bed of wool and matted leaves,
He has out-slept the winter, ventures forth
To frisk awhile, and bask in the warm sun:
He sees me, and at once, swift as a bird,
Ascends the neighbouring beech: there whisks his
　　brush,
And perks his ears, and stamps, and cries aloud,
With all the prettiness of feigned alarm,
And anger insignificantly fierce.

WILLIAM COWPER
Works, 1905

TWO RATS

He was a rat, and she was a rat
And down in one hole they did dwell,
And both were as black as a witch's cat
And they loved one another well.

He had a tail, and she had a tail
Both long and curling and fine;
And each said, "Yours is the finest tail
In the world — excepting mine."

He smelled the cheese, and she smelled the cheese,
And they both pronounced it good;
And both remarked it would greatly add
To the charms of their daily food.

So he ventured out, and she ventured out,
And I saw them go with pain,
But what befell them I never can tell
For they never came back again.

ANON

THE FIELDMOUSE

W here the acorn tumbles down,
   Where the ash tree sheds its berry,
With your fur so soft and brown,
With your eye so round and merry,
Scarcely moving the long grass,
Fieldmouse, I can see you pass.

Little thing, in what dark den,
Lie you all the winter sleeping?
Till warm weather comes again,
Then once more I see you peeping
Round about the tall tree roots,
Nibbling at their fallen fruits.

Fieldmouse, fieldmouse, do not go,
Where the farmer stacks his treasure,
Find the nut that falls below,
Eat the acorn at your pleasure,
But you must not steal the grain
He has stacked with so much pain.

Make your hole where mosses spring,
Underneath the tall oak's shadow,
Pretty, quiet, harmless thing,
Play about the sunny meadow.
Keep away from corn and house,
None will harm you, little mouse.

CECIL FRANCES ALEXANDER
Moral Songs, 1849

A LOBSTER QUADRILLE

Will you walk a little faster?" said a whiting to
    a snail,
"There's a porpoise close behind us, and he's treading
    on my tail
See how eagerly the lobsters and the turtles
    all advance!
They are waiting on the shingle — will you come
    and join the dance?
Will you, won't you, will you, won't you, will you
    join the dance?
Will you, won't you, will you, won't you, will you
    join the dance?
You can really have no notion how delightful it
    will be
When they take us up and throw us, with the
    lobsters, out to sea!"
But the snail replied, "Too far, too far!" and gave
    a look askance —

Said he thanked the whiting kindly, but he would
    not join the dance.
Would not, could not, would not, could not, could
    not join the dance.
Would not, could not, would not, could not, could
    not join the dance.
"What matters it how far we go?" his scaly friend
    replied,
"There is another shore, you know, upon the other
    side.
The further off from England, the nearer is to
    France —
Then turn not pale, beloved snail, but come and join
    the dance.
Will, you, won't you, will you, won't you, will you
    join the dance?
Will you, won't you, will you, won't you, will you
    join the dance?"

LEWIS CARROLL
Alice's Adventures in Wonderland, 1865

THE SNAIL

To grass, or leaf, or fruit, or wall,
   The Snail sticks close, nor fears to fall,
As if he grew there, house and all
Together.

Within that house secure he hides,
When danger imminent betides
Of storms, or other harm besides,
Of weather.

Give but his horns the slightest touch,
His self-collecting power is such,
He shrinks into his house with much
Displeasure.

Where'er he dwells, he dwells alone,
Except himself has chattels none,
Well satisfied to be his own
Whole treasure.

Thus hermit-like, his life he leads,
Nor partner of his Banquet needs,
And if he meets one, only feeds
The faster.

Who seeks him must be worse than blind
(He and his house are so combined)
If, finding it, he fails to find
Its master.

WILLIAM COWPER
Translations from Vincent Bourne, 1803

UPON A SNAIL

She goes but softly, but she goeth sure,
She stumbles not, as stronger creatures do;
Her journey's shorter, so she may endure
Better than they which do much further go.

She makes no noise, but stilly seizeth on
The flower or herb appointed for her food;
The which she quietly doth feed upon,
While others range, and glare, but find no good.

And though she doth but very softly go,
However slow her pace be, yet 'tis sure;
And certainly they that do travel so,
The prize which they do aim at, they procure.

JOHN BUNYAN
The Child's John Bunyan, 1929

WHISKY FRISKY

Whisky, frisky,
Hipperty hop,
Up he goes
To the tree top!

Whirly, twirly,
Round and round,
Down he scampers
To the ground.

Furly, curly,
What a tail,
Tall as a feather,
Broad as a sail.

Where's his supper?
In the shell.
Snappy, cracky,
Out it fell.

ANON

THE SQUIRREL

The winds they did blow,
The leaves they did wag;
Along came a beggar boy
And put me in his bag.
He took me to London;
A lady did me buy,
And put me in a silver cage,
And hung me up on high;
With apples by the fire,
And hazelnuts to crack,
Besides a little feather bed
To rest my tiny back.

ANON

A FRIEND IN THE GARDEN

He is not John the gardener,
  And yet the whole day long
Employs himself most usefully,
The flower beds among.

He is not Tom the pussy cat,
And yet the other day,
With stealthy stride and glistening eye,
He crept upon his prey.

He is not Dash the dear old dog,
And yet, perhaps, if you
Took pains with him and petted him,
You'd come to love him too.

He's not a blackbird, though he chirps,
And though he once was black;
And now he wears a loose grey coat,
All wrinkled on the back.

He's got a very dirty face,
And very shining eyes;
He sometimes comes and sits indoors;
He looks — and p'r'aps is — wise.

But in a sunny flower bed
He has a fixed abode;
He eats the things that eat my plants —
He is a friendly TOAD.

JULIANA HORATIA EWING
Aunt Judy's Magazine, 1873

FROG WENT A-COURTIN'

Mr. Froggie went a-courtin' an' he did ride;
Sword and pistol by his side.

He went to Missus Mousie's hall,
Gave a loud knock and gave a loud call.

"Pray, Missus Mousie, air you within?"
"Yes, kind sir, I set an' spin."

He tuk Miss Mousie on his knee,
An' sez, "Miss Mousie, will ya marry me?"

Miss Mousie blushed an' hung her head,
"You'll have t'ask Uncle Rat," she said.

"Not without Uncle Rat's consent
Would I marry the Pres-i-dent."

Uncle Rat jumped up an' shuck his fat side,
To think his niece would be Bill Frog's bride.

Nex' day Uncle Rat went to town,
To git his niece a weddin' gown.

Whar shall the weddin' supper be?
'Way down yander in a holler tree.

First come in was a Bumble-bee,
Who danced a jig with Captain Flea.

Next come in was a Butterfly,
Sellin' butter very high.

An' when they all set down to sup,
A big gray goose come an' gobbled 'em all up.

An' this is the end of one, two, three,
The Rat an' the Mouse an' the little Froggie.

ANON

FEATHERED FRIENDS

THE CROW

Old Crow, upon the tall tree-top
I see you sitting at your ease,
You hang upon the highest bough
And balance in the breeze.

How many miles you've been to-day
Upon your wing so strong and black,
And steered across the dark grey sky
Without a guide or track;

Above the city wrapped in smoke,
Green fields and rivers flowing clear;
Now tell me, as you passed them o'er,
What did you see and hear?

The old crow shakes his sooty wing
And answers hoarsely, "Caw, caw, caw,"
And that is all the crow can tell
Of what he heard and saw.

CECIL FRANCES ALEXANDER
Moral Songs, 1849

CUCKOO

Cuckoo, cuckoo
What do you do?
In April,
I open my bill;
In May,
I sing night and day;
In June,
I change my tune;
In July,
Away I fly;
In August,
Go I must.

ANON

THE OWL

When cats run home and light is come,
    And dew is cold upon the ground,
And the far-off stream is dumb,
And the whirring sail goes round,
And the whirring sail goes round;
Alone and warming his five wits,
The white owl in the belfry sits.

When merry milkmaids click the latch,
And rarely smells the new-mown hay,
And the cock hath sung beneath the thatch
Twice or thrice his roundelay,
Twice or thrice his roundelay;
Alone and warming his five wits,
The white owl in the belfry sits.

ALFRED, LORD TENNYSON
Juvenalia, 1830

Little Trotty Wagtail, he went in the rain,
  And tittering tottering sideways, he ne'er got
    straight again,
He stooped to get a worm, and looked up to catch
    a fly,
And then he flew away ere his feathers they were dry.

Little Trotty Wagtail, he waddled in the mud,
And left his little footmarks, trample where he
    would.
He waddled in the water-pudge, and waggle went
    his tail,
And chirruped up his wings to dry upon the
    garden rail.

Little Trotty Wagtail, you nimble all about,
And in the dimpling water-pudge, you waddle in
    and out;
Your home is nigh at hand, and in the warm pig-sty,
So, little Master Wagtail, I'll bid you a good-bye.

JOHN CLARE

THE PARROT

I am the pirate's parrot,
I sail the seven seas
And sleep inside the crow's nest
Don't look for me in trees!

I am the pirate's parrot,
A bird both brave and bold.
I guard the captain's treasure
And count his hoard of gold.

ANON

THE SWALLOW

Fly away, fly away, over the sea,
Sun-loving swallow, for summer is done.
Come again, come again, come back to me,
Bringing the summer and bringing the sun.

CHRISTINA ROSSETTI
Sing-Song, 1872

THE VULTURE

The Vulture eats between his meals
  And that's the reason why
He very, very rarely feels
As well as you and I.

His eye is dull, his head is bald,
His neck is growing thinner.
Oh! what a lesson for us all
To only eat at dinner!

HILAIRE BELLOC
More Beasts for Worse Children, 1897

THE BIRDS

Do you ask what the birds say?
The sparrow, the dove,
The linnet, and thrush say:
I love and I love.

In the Winter they're silent,
The wind is so strong;
What it says I don't know,
But it sings a loud song.

But green leaves and blossoms,
And sunny, warm weather,
And singing and loving,
All come back together.

Then the lark is so brimful
Of gladness and love,
The green fields below him,
The blue sky above,

That he sings and he sings,
And for ever sings he:
I love my love,
And my love loves me.

SAMUEL TAYLOR COLERIDGE

THE SANDPIPER

Across the lonely beach we flit,
One little sandpiper and I;
And fast I gather, bit by bit,
The scattered driftwood, bleached and dry.
The wild waves reach their hands for it,
The wild wind raves, the tide runs high,
As up and down the beach we flit —
One little sandpiper and I.

Above our heads the sullen clouds
Scud black and swift across the sky;
Like silent ghosts in misty shrouds
Stand out the white lighthouses high.
Almost as far as eye can reach
I see the close-reefed vessels fly,
As fast we flit along the beach —
One little sandpiper and I.

I watch him as he skims along
Uttering his sweet and mournful cry;
He starts not at my fitful song
Or flash of fluttering drapery.
He has no thought of any wrong,
He scans me with a fearless eye;
Staunch friends are we, well-tried and strong,
The little sandpiper and I.

Comrade, where wilt thou be tonight
When the loosed storm breaks furiously?
My driftwood fire will burn so bright!
To what warm shelter canst thou fly?
I do not fear for thee, though wroth
The tempest rushes through the sky:
For are we not God's children both,
Thou, little sandpiper, and I?

CELIA THAXTER
Poems, 1872

BEASTS AND BIRDS

The dog will come when he is called,
  The cat will walk away;
The monkey's cheek is very bald,
The goat is fond of play.
The parrot is a prate-apace,
Yet knows not what she says;
The noble horse will win the race,
Or draw you in a chaise.

The pig is not a feeder nice,
The squirrel loves a nut,
The wolf would eat you in a trice,
The buzzard's eyes are shut.
The lark sings high up in the air,
The linnet in the tree;
The swan he has a bosom fair,
And who so proud as he?

ADELAIDE O'KEEFE
Poems For Infant Minds, Vol. II, 1805

THE SEA-GULL

The waves leap up, the wild wind blows,
And the Gulls together crowd,
And wheel about, and madly scream
To the deep sea roaring loud.
And let the sea roar ever so loud,
And the wind pipe ever so high,
With a wilder joy the bold Sea-gull
Sends forth a wilder cry.

For the Sea-gull, he is a daring bird,
And he loves with the storm to sail;
To ride in the strength of the billowy sea,
And to breast the driving gale!
The little boat, she is tossed about,
Like a sea-weed, to and fro;
The tall ship reels like a drunken man,
As the gusty tempests blow.

But the Sea-gull laughs at the fear of man,
And sails in a wild delight
On the torn-up breast of the night-black sea,
Like a foam cloud, calm and white.
The waves may rage and the winds may roar,
But he fears not wreck nor need;
For he rides the sea, in its stormy strength,
As a strong man rides his steed.

Oh, the white Sea-gull, the bold Sea-gull!
He makes on the shore his nest,
And he tries what the inland fields may be;
But he loveth the sea the best!
And away from land a thousand leagues,
He goes 'mid surging foam;
What matter to him is land or shore,
For the sea is his truest home!

MARY HOWITT
excerpt, Birds and Flowers, 1838

THE ROOKS

The rooks are building on the trees;
They build there every spring:
"Caw, caw," is all they say,
For none of them can sing.

They're up before the break of day,
And up till late at night;
For they must labour busily
As long as it is light.

And many a crooked stick they bring,
And many a slender twig,
And many a tuft of moss, until
Their nests are round and big.

"Caw, caw." Oh, what a noise
They make in rainy weather!
Good children always speak by turns,
But rooks all talk together.

JANE EUPHEMIA BROWNE
Aunt Effie's Rhymes For Little Children, 1852

A WARNING

The robin and the redbreast,
　The robin and the wren,
If you take them from their nests,
Ye'll ne'er thrive again.

The robin and the redbreast,
The martin and the swallow,
If you touch one of their eggs,
Ill luck is sure to follow.

ANON

BED-TIME

Robin Friend has gone to bed,
　Little wing to hide his head.
Mother's bird must slumber, too —
Just as baby robins do.
When the stars begin to rise
Birds and Babies close their eyes.

L. ALMA TADEMA
Realms of Unknown Kings, 1897

The fireside for the cricket,
  The wheatstack for the mouse,
When trembling night-winds whistle
And moan all round the house;
The frosty ways like iron,
The branches plumed with snow —
Alas! in winter, dead and dark,
Where can poor Robin go?
Robin, Robin Redbreast,
O Robin dear!
And a crumb of bread for Robin,
His little heart to cheer.

WILLIAM ALLINGHAM
Fifty Modern Poems, 1865

THE BOY AND THE PARROT

Parrot, if I had your wings
    I should do so many things:
I should fly to Uncle Bartle,
Don't you think 'twould make him startle,
If he saw me when I came,
Flapping at the window frame
Exactly like the parrot of fame?"

All this the wise old parrot heard,
The parrot was an ancient bird,
And paused and pondered every word;
First, therefore, he began to cough,
He paused awhile, and coughed again:
"Master John, pray think a little,
What will you do for beds and victual?"

"Oh! parrot, Uncle John can tell —
But we should manage very well;
At night we'd perch upon the trees,
And so fly forward by degrees."

"Does Uncle John," the parrot said,
"Put nonsense in his nephew's head?
I think he might have taught you better,
You might have learnt to write a letter:
That is the thing that I should do
If I had little hands like you."

JOHN HOOKHAM FRERE
excerpt, Fables for Five Years Old, 1830

THE BLOSSOM

Merry, merry sparrow!
Under leaves so green
A happy blossom
Sees you swift as arrow
Seek your cradle narrow
Near my bosom.

Pretty, pretty robin!
Under leaves so green
A happy blossom
Hears you sobbing, sobbing,
Pretty, pretty robin,
Near my bosom.

WILLIAM BLAKE
Songs of Innocence, 1789

I SOMETIMES THINK
I'D RATHER CROW

I sometimes think I'd rather crow
And be a rooster than to roost
And be a crow. But I dunno.

A rooster he can roost also,
Which don't seem fair when crows can't crow.
Which may help some. Still I dunno.

Crows should be glad of one thing though;
Nobody thinks of eating crow,
While roosters they are good enough
For anyone unless they're tough.

There're lots of tough old roosters though,
And anyway a crow can't crow,
So mebby roosters stand more show.
It looks that way. But I dunno.

ANON

THE KING-FISHER SONG

King Fisher courted Lady Bird —
  Sing Beans, sing Bones, sing Butterflies!
  "Find me my match," he said,
  "With such a noble head —
With such a beard, as white as curd —
  With such expressive eyes!"

"Yet pins have heads," said Lady Bird —
Sing Prunes, sing Prawns, sing Primrose-Hill!
  "And, where you stick them in,
  They stay, and thus a pin
Is very much to be preferred
  To one that's never still!"

"Oysters have beards," said Lady Bird —
Sing Flies, sing Frogs, sing Fiddle-strings!
  "I love them, for I know
  They never chatter so:
They would not say one single word —
  Not if you crowned them Kings!"

"Needles have eyes," said Lady Bird —
Sing Cats, sing Corks, sing Cowslip-tea!
  "And they are sharp — just what
  Your Majesty is *not*:
So get you gone — 'tis too absurd
  To come a-courting *me!*"

                    LEWIS CARROLL

The dove says, "Coo,
What shall I do?
I can hardly maintain my two."
"Pooh," says the wren,
"Why, I've got ten
And keep them all like gentlemen!"

ANON

COCK ROBIN

Who killed Cock Robin?
"I," said the Sparrow,
"With my bow and arrow,
I killed Cock Robin."

Who saw him die?
"I," said the Fly,
"With my little eye,
I saw him die."

Who caught his blood?
"I," said the Fish,
"With my little dish,
I caught his blood."

Who'll make his shroud?
"I," said the Beetle,
"With my thread and needle,
I'll make his shroud·"

Who'll dig his grave?
"I," said the Owl,
"With my spade and trowel,
I'll dig his grave."

Who'll be the parson?
"I," said the Rook,
"With my little book,
I'll be the parson."

Who'll be the clerk?
"I," said the Lark,
"I'll say Amen in the dark;
I'll be the clerk."

Who'll be chief mourner?
"I," said the Dove,
"I mourn for my love;
I'll be chief mourner."

Who'll bear the torch?
"I," said the Linnet,
"I'll come in a minute,
I'll bear the torch."

Who'll sing his dirge?
"I," said the Thrush,
"As I sing in the bush
I'll sing his dirge."

Who'll bear the pall?
"We," said the Wren,
Both the Cock and the Hen;
"We'll bear the pall."

Who'll carry his coffin?
"I," said the Kite,
"If it be in the night,
I'll carry his coffin."

Who'll toll the bell?
"I," said the Bull,
"Because I can pull,
I'll toll the bell."

All the birds of the air
Fell to sighing and sobbing
When they heard the bell toll
For poor Cock Robin.

ANON

SMALLEST
CREATURES

THE FLY

Little fly,
Thy summer's play
My thoughtless hand
Has brushed away

Am not I
A fly like thee?
Or art not thou
A man like me?

For I dance
And drink and sing
Till some blind hand
Shall brush my wing

If thought is life
And strength and breath
And the want
Of thought is death,

Then am I
A happy fly,
If I live
Or if I die.

WILLIAM BLAKE
Songs of Experience, 1794

L adybird, ladybird, fly away home;
  Thy house is on fire, thy children all gone —
All but one, and her name is Ann,
And she crept under the pudding-pan.

ANON

THE QUEEN BEE

When I was in the garden,
  I saw a great Queen Bee;
She was the very largest one
That I did ever see.
She wore a shiny helmet
And a lovely velvet gown,
But I was rather sad, because
She didn't wear a crown.

MARY K. ROBINSON

CATERPILLAR

Brown and furry
Caterpillar in a hurry,
Take your walk
To the shady leaf, or stalk,
Or what not,
Which may be the chosen spot.
No toad spy you,
Hovering bird of prey pass by you;
Spin and die,
To live again a butterfly.

CHRISTINA ROSSETTI
Sing-Song, 1872

Swarms of minnows show their little heads,
Staying their wavy bodies 'gainst the streams,
To taste the luxury of sunny beams
Tempered with coolness. How they ever wrestle
With their own sweet delight, and ever nestle
Their silver bellies on the pebbly sand.
If you but scantily hold out the hand,
That very instant not one will remain;
But turn your eye, and they are there again.

JOHN KEATS

A NOISELESS PATIENT SPIDER

A noiseless patient spider,
I mark'd where on a little promontory it stood
 isolated,
Mark'd how to explore the vacant vast surrounding,
It launch'd forth filament, filament, filament, out
 of itself,
Ever unreeling them, ever tirelessly speeding them.

And you O my soul where you stand,
Surrounded, detached, in measureless oceans
 of space,
Ceaselessly musing, venturing, throwing, seeking
 the spheres to connect them,
Till the bridge you will need be form'd, till the
 ductile anchor hold,
Till the gossamer thread you fling catch somewhere,
 O my soul.

WALT WHITMAN
Leaves Of Grass, 1855

Great fleas have little fleas upon their backs to bite 'em,
And little fleas have lesser fleas, and so ad infinitum.
And the great fleas themselves in turn have greater fleas to go on
While these again have greater still, and greater still, and so on.

A. DE MORGAN

Today I saw the dragon-fly
Come from the wells where he did lie.

An inner impulse rent the veil
Of his old husk: from head to tail
Came out clear plates of sapphire mail.

He dried his wings: like gauze they grew;
Through crofts and pastures wet with dew
A living flash of light, he flew.

ALFRED, LORD TENNYSON

THE POETS

ALEXANDER, Cecil Frances
(1818-1895) Ireland
Born in Co. Wicklow, Ireland. In 1850 she married the Rev. William Alexander, who was to become Archbishop of Armagh.
Hymns for Little Children (1848) includes not only "All Things Bright and Beautiful" but also "Once in Royal David's City" and "There is a Green Hill Far Away."

ALLINGHAM, William
(1824-1889) Ireland
Born in Ballyshannon in Donegal, Allingham spent most of his life working as a customs officer. His great love for the literature and the peasantry of his native land inspired him to write.

ALMA-TADEMA, Laurence
(1865-1940) UK
Daughter of the pre-Raphaelite painter Sir Lawrence Alma-Tadema and a close friend of the pianist and politician Paderewski, Alma-Tadema died a spinster, as she had prophesied in her famous poem *If No-one Ever Marries Me* (1897).

BELLOC, Joseph Hilaire Pierre
(1870-1953) France
Historian, poet, essayist, novelist, and traveler. Belloc was born near Paris, but was forced to flee with his mother to England by the Franco-Prussian war. An astoundingly prolific author, his more celebrated works include *A Bad Child's Book of Beasts* (1896) and *More Beasts* (1897), from which the verses in this collection are taken; *Danton* (1899); *The Path to Rome* (1902); *Cautionary Tales for Children* (1907); *The French Revolution* (1911); and *The Cruise of "the Nona"* (1925). A devout Catholic and a great friend of G.K. Chesterton (q.v.), he left an enormous legacy of works characterized by intellectual vigor, euphony, contentiousness, and down-to-earth spirituality.

BLAKE, William
(1757-1827) UK
Poet, painter, and visionary, Blake had no formal education but served an apprenticeship with an engraver. In 1789 he published his *Songs of Innocence*, decorated with his own engravings, then the radical prose work *The Marriage of Heaven and Hell* (1790) and the *Songs of Experience* (1794). A great craftsman and a compulsive worker, Blake wrote verses of deceptive simplicity and sweetness which reveal, however, much righteous anger and fierce idealism.

BROWNE, Jane Euphemia (Aunt Effie)
(1811-1898) UK
Jane Euphemia Browne lived the respectable, restricted life of the well-born, well-to-do Victorian lady, but enjoyed another, secret life in the persona of "Aunt Effie," an enormously popular children's writer and author of *Aunt Effie's Rhymes for Little Children* (1852) and *Aunt Effie's Gift for the Nursery* (1854). She married Stephen Saxby, a Somerset vicar.

BUNYAN, John
(1628-1688) UK
Drafted into Cromwell's parliamentary army, Bunyan devoted much of his life to a study of the bible. In 1660 he was arrested for preaching without a license and remained in prison for twelve years, during which he wrote many books; *Grace Abounding to the Chief of Sinners* (1666) and *The Holy City* (1666) being most important. He was released in 1672, but was again arrested. During this period he wrote the first part of his famous *Pilgrim's Progress* (1678). *The Holy War* was published in 1682.

CARROLL, Lewis (Charles Lutwidge Dodgson)
(1832-1898) UK
Lewis Carroll rapidly became famous for his two great works of fantasy and distorted logic, *Alice's Adventures in Wonderland* (1865) and *Through the Looking-glass* (1872), but he was already celebrated in academic circles as a lecturer in mathematics at Oxford. Queen Victoria, expressing her admiration for *Alice*, asked Carroll for a copy of his next book and was dismayed to receive a learned tome about Euclidian geometry.

CARRYL, Charles Edward
(1841-1920) USA
Carryl was a New York businessman who ran railroad companies in a single-minded manner until one day he came upon a copy of *Alice's Adventures in Wonderland*. Inspired by this he began to write fantasy stories interspersed with verses for his own children. The best of these are *Davy and the Goblin* (1886) and *The Admiral's Caravan* (1892).

CHESTERTON, Gilbert Keith
(1874-1936) UK

Poet, novelist, critic, and artist, Chesterton was extraordinarily prolific. Among his works are full-length studies of Dickens, Browning, Stevenson, and St. Thomas Aquinas. He is principally famous, however, for the Father Brown stories. A stubborn and formidable writer, Chesterton was otherwise renowned for his bumbling absent-mindedness and his unfailing ability to get lost.

CLARE, John
(1793-1864) UK

The son of a laborer, rural poet Clare led a picaresque life, his various occupations being listed as "herd-boy, militiaman, vagrant, and unsuccessful farmer." In 1837, after four volumes of his verse had been published, he was declared insane.

COLERIDGE, Samuel Taylor
(1772-1834) UK

Coleridge was a romantic poet, mystic, critic, and scholar. The son of a Devonshire vicar, Coleridge was briefly a soldier, but from 1794 onward concentrated entirely on political reform, journalism, and verse. *Lyrical Ballads* (1798) by Coleridge and his friend Wordsworth (q.v.) contains "Rime of the Ancient Mariner." Other famous poems by Coleridge include "Christabel" (1816) and "Kubla Khan" (1816), though these were in fact far earlier works and, by the time of their publication, the poet's health had been broken by opium.

COWPER, William
(1731-1800) UK

Originally trained as a solicitor, Cowper disliked the law and gave it up. He wrote several well-known hymns, some satires, and the well-known "John Gilpin" (1782), "The Task" (1784), and short poems such as "To Mary" (1802). Cowper's style reflects the simplicity of his nature and marks a transition from the formal classicism of the eighteenth century to the freer forms of the nineteenth century.

DICKINSON, Emily Elizabeth
(1830-1886) USA

The daughter of a wealthy lawyer from Amherst, Massachusetts, Emily Dickinson lived the quiet life of a respectable, intellectual spinster. She had several very intelligent male friends, but was otherwise a recluse for the last twenty-five years of her life. No one knew until she died that she had written more than a thousand poems of remarkable sensitivity and originality. Like the English naturalist Gilbert White, she expressed the sharp, ecstatic pangs occasioned by everyday things precisely observed. Her images were eccentric, witty, and concise.

EMERSON, Ralph Waldo
(1803-1882) USA

Essayist, philosopher, and poet, Emerson was born in America but came to England in 1833, meeting Coleridge (q.v.), Wordsworth (q.v.) and many other prominent poets. His first great work, *Nature* (1836), was a philosophical essay. Many of his early poems appeared in *The Dial*, of which he was editor. His *Essays* were published in 1841 and 1844, his *Poems* in 1847, and his *Journals* from 1909-1914.

EWING, Juliana Horatia (née Gatty)
(1841-1885) UK

Daughter of the founder of the successful children's monthly *Aunt Judy's Magazine*, Juliana Ewing rapidly became the magazine's principal contributor of verses and stories. Her best known work is *The Miller's Thumb* (1873), republished as *Jan of the Windmill* (1884).

FIELD, Eugene
(1850-1895) USA

Born in St. Louis, Missouri, Field was a columnist with the *Chicago Morning News*, contributing literary and humorous pieces or light verse. His most well known poem, "Wynken Blynken and Nod", was written in bed "upon brown wrapping paper" one night in March 1889 when the entire poem suddenly came into his head.

FRERE, John Hookham
(1769-1846) UK

As a diplomat, Frere served as British envoy to Lisbon (1800-02), Madrid (1802-04), and the Junta (1808-09). He was also one of the founders of two important periodicals of his time, *The Microcosm* (1786-7) and the *Quarterly Review*.

GAY, John
(1685-1732) UK

Balladeer and playwright, Gay was principally famous for two works, *The Beggar's Opera* (1728) and its sequel *Polly* (1729).

GRAHAME, Kenneth
(1859-1922) UK
Grahame's first successful work was *The Golden Age* (1895), a nostalgic collection of studies of childhood, then came *Dream Days* (1898), and the much-loved children's classic *The Wind in the Willows* (1908), in which the perennial favorites Toad, Ratty, Mole, and Badger first saw the light of day.

HARDY, Thomas
(1840-1928) UK
Initially an architect, poet and novelist Hardy wrote a large number of very popular novels about his native Dorset, including *Tess of the d'Urbervilles* (1891) and *Jude the Obscure* (1895). He regarded fiction, however, merely as a means of making a living, and longed instead to write verse. After the publication of *Jude the Obscure* he gave up novel-writing and devoted the rest of his life to poetry. Although they use conventional forms, Hardy's poems are startlingly original in tone and syntax.

HOWELLS, William Dean
(1837-1920) USA
American novelist and critic, Howells was the editor of the *Atlantic Monthly* (1872) and associate editor of *Harper's Magazine* (1886-91). He was a prolific writer of literary articles and of romances.

HOWITT, Mary (née Botham)
(1799-1888) UK
Wife of author William Howitt and mother of twelve children, Mary Howitt, a Quaker, collaborated with her husband and published more than a hundred books in her own right. Among other claims to fame, she was the first English translator of Hans Christian Andersen.

KEATS, John
(1795-1821) UK
The son of a livery stable-keeper in London, Keats was apprenticed to an apothecary but turned instead to surgery before his enthusiasm for literature got the better of him. His great sonnet "On First Looking into Chapman's Homer" was published by Leigh Hunt in the *Examiner* in 1816, to be followed by "The Poems" of 1817. Then came "Endymion" (1818) and a host of great poems, including "The Eve of St. Agnes," "La Belle Dame Sans Merci," and the magnificent autumn odes, "On a Grecian Urn," "To A Nightingale," "To Autumn," and "On Melancholy." Keats died of tuberculosis in 1821,

one of the greatest of English poets and letter-writers.

KIPLING, (Joseph) Rudyard
(1865-1936) UK
Born in Bombay and educated in England, Kipling returned to India in 1882 and rapidly acquired a reputation as a brilliant reporter and satirical poet. He settled in London in 1889. His most popular works include *The Jungle Books* (1894 and 5), *Stalky and Co.* (1899), *Kim* (1901), and *Just So Stories* (1902). He was a fine wordsmith; "A word." he said, "should fall in its place like a bell in a full chime."

LEAR, Edward
(1812-1888) UK
Principally known as the father of nonsense verse and chief exponent of the limerick, Lear was also a considerable traveler and so fine a painter that he was invited to teach Queen Victoria to paint in watercolors. His *Book of Nonsense* (1846) was written for the grandchildren of his patron, the Earl of Derby.

LUCAS, Edward Verrall
(1868-1938) UK
Essayist and biographer – and one-time assistant editor of *Punch*, Lucas wrote a biography of Charles Lamb and edited his works and letters. Aside from these, his best-known writing is contained in the light works *The Open Road* (1899) and *The Friendly Town* (1905).

MARVELL, Andrew
(1621-1678) UK
Marvell made his living principally as a private tutor, first to the daughter of Lord Fairfax, then to the son of Oliver Cromwell's ward, William Dutton. In 1657 he became John Milton's assistant and wrote several poems in praise of both Milton and Cromwell. His poems, which include "To His Coy Mistress" and "The Garden," were not published until 1681.

MELVILLE, Herman
(1819-1891) USA
Born in New York, Melville had perhaps the most adventurous life of all the modern writers. A sailor, he served on the whaler *Dolly* and, in 1842, having rounded Cape Horn, abandoned his ship and its brutal captain and sought refuge in the Marquesas Islands. Here he and his friend were held captive by the cannibal tribe, the Typees.

He recounted this tale in *Typee, a Peep at Polynesian Life* (1846). His greatest book, however, is the tale of Captain Ahab's obsessive hunt of the great white whale in *Moby Dick* (1851).

DE MORGAN, Mary Augusta
(1850-1907) UK
Sister of the pre-Raphaelite William de Morgan, Mary Augusta de Morgan wrote several collection of fairy stories, such as *On a Pincushion and other Fairy Tales* (1877) and *The Windfairies and other Tales* (1900).

O'KEEFE, Adelaide
(1776-1855) UK
Like the Taylors, Adelaide O'Keefe contributed to the collection *Original Poems for Infant Minds*. Although a collection of her own poems. *Original Poems: Calculated to Improve the Mind of Youth*, was also published, O'Keefe spent most of her life caring for her blind father.

RANDS, William Brighty
(1823-1882) UK
Rand was a self-educated children's poet who was born and spent most of his life in or about West London.

RILEY, James Whitcomb
(1849-1916) USA
A Hoosier poet renowned for his absent-minded eccentricity, Riley was born in Greenfield, Indiana and remained forever loyal to his birthplace. He became one of the United States' best-loved poets, particularly for "Little Orphan Annie" (1886). In 1912 children in schools throughout America celebrated his birthday.

ROSSETTI, Christina Georgina
(1830-1894) UK
Sister of the poet and painter Dante Gabriel Rossetti, Christina led a sad life and failed to fulfill her early exceptional promise. She twice rejected suitors because of her high Anglican religious principles, and her verses are devout and full of the sadness of "what might have been." Her first collection, *Goblin Market* (1862), is her finest, but *Sing-Song* (1872) is full of charming, simple verses for children. She was always frail and, at the time of *Sing-Song's* composition, was very close to death from Grave's disease. Thereafter she taught with her mother and wrote "morally improving" verse.

STEVENSON, Robert Louis
(1850-1894) USA
Stevenson was a master stylist and supremely imaginative writer who contrived to lead a hero's life despite often crippling illness. All his life he suffered from chronic bronchial problems and acute nervous excitability. Stevenson nonetheless traveled extensively, wrote many fine essays and novels, and in *A Child's Garden of Verses* (1885) applied his highly developed gifts of imagination and sympathy to the emotions and enthusiasms of childhood. In so doing he can be said to have invented a whole new genre of verse. In 1888 he traveled to the South Seas and at last settled with his family in Samoa, where the natives called him "Tusitala" (the tale-teller). He died there of a brain hemorrhage. His novels include *Treasure Island* (1883), *Kidnapped* (1886), *Catriona* (1893), and for older readers the eerie *Strange Case of Dr. Jekyll and Mr. Hyde* (1886).

TAYLOR, Jane and Ann
(1783-1824) UK
With her sister Ann, Jane Taylor was the best known children's poet of her time. They lived together at their family home in Colchester, Essex.

TENNYSON, Alfred, Lord
(1809-1892) UK
Although the most honored poet of the Victorian era, Tennyson liked to live "far from the madding crowd" in Hampshire or on the Isle of Wight. He was very prolific and although he never wrote specifically for children, many of his works have become firm favorites with young people because of their grand romantic subject matter or because they are ideal for reciting.

THACKERAY, William Makepeace
(1811-1863) UK
Originally a lawyer, then an artist, Thackeray started to contribute pieces to *Punch* in 1842. His finest book, *Vanity Fair*, was published in monthly numbers from 1847 to 1848, then came *The History of Pendennis* (1848-50), *Esmond* (1852), *The Newcomes* (1853-55), and *The Virginians* (1857-59).

THAXTER, Celia (née Laighton)
(1835-1894) USA
Born in Portsmouth, New Hampshire, Thaxter's father was an ambitious politician. When he failed to be elected state governor, he decided on a whim to be a lighthouse-keeper. Celia, therefore, who had been used to a rich world with

lots of company, now found herself growing up with her two brothers and a lot of seabirds on the Isle of Shoals, ten miles from the mainland. She married and moved back to the mainland, but in 1866 returned to the solitude of her beloved islands.

THOMPSON, D'Arcy Wentworth

(1829-1902) UK
Thompson was a Classics Master at Edinburgh University, where his pupils included Robert Louis Stevenson. He wrote *Nursery Nonsense or Rymes without Reason* (1864) for his small son.

WHITMAN, Walt

(1819-1892) USA
Initially a printer and only an occasional writer, Whitman seemed set for a successful career as an editor, but his political integrity hindered him and he found himself earning a living as a carpenter and builder until he published the startlingly original *Leaves of Grass* in 1855. At first ill-received, it slowly grew in popularity until his then employer — the government — became aware of their lowly clerk's part-time job and dismissed him on the grounds of the book's "immorality." This caused a furor which at once sold many copies of the book and helped Whitman earn the enormous reputation he enjoys today.

WORDSWORTH, William

(1770-1850) UK
The poet laureate lived at Grasmere in the English Lake District with his sister Dorothy. At his best, as in "The Prelude" or "Tintern Abbey," Wordsworth was a brilliant, thoughtful nature poet; at his worst he was capable of gaucheness and banality.

YEATS, William Butler

(1865-1939) Ireland
Born in Dublin, Ireland, Yeats was the guiding genius behind the establishment of the Irish National Theatre Company. Yeats's marvelous lyrical verse and ballads are contained in a host of collections, from *Poems* (1895) to *The Winding Stair* (1933).

THE PAINTERS

INDEX OF FIRST LINES